Goes to The Vet

NICK BRUEL

SQUARE
FISH

A NEAL PORTER BOOK
ROARING BROOK PRESS
NEW YORK

SQUARE
FISH

An imprint of Macmillan Publishing Group, LLC
175 Fifth Avenue
New York, NY 10010
mackids.com

Square Fish and the Square Fish logo are trademarks of Macmillan and
are used by Roaring Brook Press under license from Macmillan.

Our books may be purchased in bulk for promotional, educational, or business use. Please
contact your local bookseller or the Macmillan Corporate and Premium Sales Department at
(800) 221-7945 ext. 5442 or by e-mail at MacmillanSpecialMarkets@macmillan.com.

Library of Congress Cataloging-in-Publication Data

Bruel, Nick.
    Bad kitty goes to the vet / Nick Bruel.
        pages cm. — (Bad kitty)
    "A Neal Porter Book."
    Summary: "Even the best bad kitties can get sick, and when it happens, it means just one
thing: a visit to the vet!"— Provided by publisher.
    ISBN 978-1-250-10380-2 (paperback)
[1. Cats—Fiction. 2. Veterinarians—Fiction. 3. Humorous stories.] I. Title.
PZ7.B82832Baj 2016
    [E]—dc23

                                                                                    2015014997

Special Book Fair Edition ISBN 978-1-62672-580-5

Originally published in the United States by Neal Porter Books/Roaring Brook Press
First Square Fish Edition: 2017
Square Fish logo designed by Filomena Tuosto

1 3 5 7 9 10 8 6 4 2

AR: 3.4 / LEXILE: 600L

• CONTENTS •

CHAPTER ONE
POOR, SICK KITTY 5

CHAPTER TWO
HOW TO TAKE KITTY
TO THE VET 26

CHAPTER THREE
AT THE VET 52

CHAPTER FOUR
PUSSYCAT PARADISE 72

CHAPTER FIVE
HOME AGAIN 96

POOR, SICK KITTY

This is what Kitty looks like when she's a happy, healthy pussycat.

She has lots of energy.

She has a good appetite.

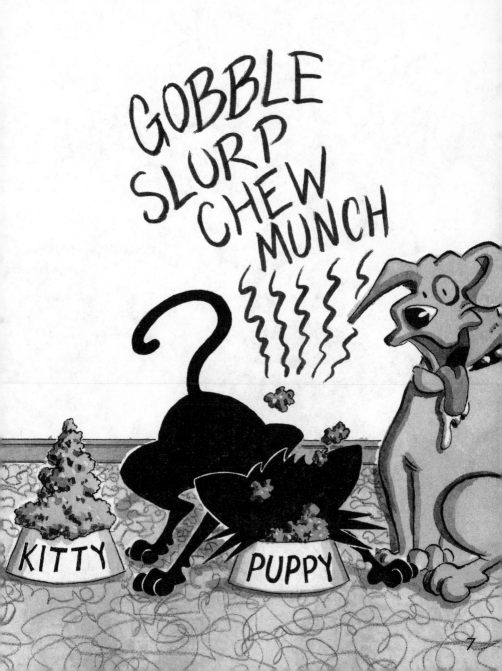

She has a really, REALLY good appetite.

And she keeps herself nice and clean.

But that's not how Kitty looks today. She looks terrible. She looks tired. She looks unhappy. She does not look healthy at all.

GROAN

And worst of all . . . Kitty is just not eating her food.

Kitty, I don't understand why you're not eating. I've watched grown men cry trying to beat you at a hot dog eating contest. I once saw you swallow an entire liver and pineapple pizza in one gulp. I've seen you consume an entire meatloaf the size of a car in just five minutes. It was horrifying.

This is the warning poster that hangs over the meat counter of every grocery store in the county.

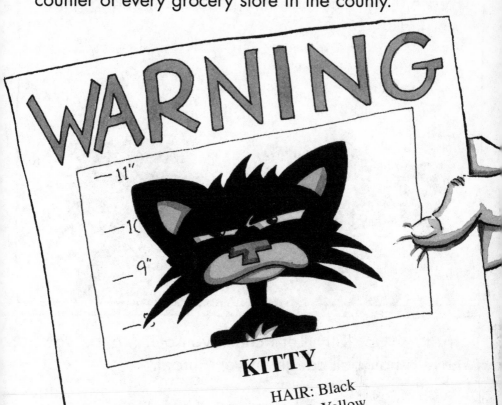

KITTY

HEIGHT: 11″
WEIGHT: 8.5 lbs.

HAIR: Black
EYES: Yellow

This hungry feline felon has been known to distract innocent butchers with soulful eyes and a sequence of sad meows until she suddenly devours all stock in a matter of minutes.

Do not attempt to engage. Feline is heavily armed with claws, sharp teeth, and projectile hair balls.

Call police, animal control, and air force if nasty, violent feline is sighted.

But today you're not even touching your breakfast! Please, Kitty! Eat something! You're starting to get us worried.

Try to sit up, Kitty. Let's check you out. Maybe you have a hair ball caught in your throat.

Nothing? Hmmmm . . . I think I should feel your belly just to see if you have any lumps.

Hold still, Kitty. I promise this won't hurt one bit.

HEE-YUK! BWAH-HEE-HAR-HAR-HA! HO-HEE-HO-HAR-HEE-HAR-HA!

16

Sorry about that, Kitty. I honestly had no idea you were so ticklish.

I think that maybe it's time to take your temperature, Kitty.

Uhhhh . . . Sorry, Kitty. It's not that kind of thermo-meter.

That is not helpful, Kitty.

Look, Kitty, you're obviously not feeling well, and we have no idea what's wrong. But we know that something IS wrong. It could be serious. It could be nothing. But if you're not going to let me take your temperature, then someone else will have to.

I guess we're just going to have to take you to the . . .

VET.

Great.
Well, I guess she has a little energy left in her after all.

UNCLE MURRAY'S FUN FACTS

HOW CAN YOU TELL IF A CAT IS SICK?

They're all pretty sick in the head if you ask me! HAR! HAR!

Trying to figure out if a cat is sick is no laughing matter.

Sorry.

Cats can get sick in the same way that people can get sick with everything from the common cold to heart disease. But the obvious problem is that cats cannot tell you themselves if they're not feeling well, so YOU have to be aware of any signs they might show in their physical appearance or their behavior.

Does your cat LOOK sick?

Does your cat have a runny nose or runny eyes?

Is your cat scratching her ears excessively?

When you pet your cat, do you feel odd bumps under her fur or her skin?

Does your cat's fur look messy or dirty when usually it looks smooth and clean?

Is your cat breathing funny?

Is your cat ACTING sick?

- Is your cat using the litter box a lot more or a lot less than usual?

- Is your cat acting dizzy or is she tilting her head to one side a lot?

- Is your cat not eating or even losing weight?

- Look for any sudden change in your cat's personality. If your cat is very active one day but acts unusually tired the next day, there might be a problem.

Sometimes cats will get better all on their own—just like people. But sometimes the problem can be quite serious.

If you even THINK your cat might be sick, the safest thing to do is bring her to an expert who can figure out what is wrong and what to do. And that expert is a veterinarian.

Don't take chances with someone else's health. That's my motto.

•CHAPTER TWO•

HOW TO TAKE KITTY TO THE VET

The following is a list of the Top 10 things cats hate the most.

#10: Spiders

#9: Empty Bowls

#8: Closed Doors

#7: You

#6: Doorbells

#5: Nail Clippers

#4: Other Cats

#3: Dogs

#2: Veterinarians

#1: Baths

Please note that veterinarians are #2 on this list and that war, homework, and parking tickets do not appear on this list at all.

This means that when it's time for your cat to go to the vet, your cat will really, really, really (*insert the word "really" 1,394,291 more times here*) not want to go to the vet.

This is what happened the last three times we brought Kitty to the vet.

Please follow these five very important steps when taking a cat to the vet so you can both come out of this alive. Well . . . mostly so YOU can come out of this alive.

•STEP ONE•
GATHER YOUR EQUIPMENT

This is what you will need to bring your cat to the vet.

That's it. That is all you will need to bring your cat to the vet. A cat carrier.

BUT . . .

The following is what you will need to get your cat **INTO** the cat carrier . . .

Gloves made out of the same stuff they use to make bulletproof vests.

Treats

Padding and duct tape. Lots and lots of padding and duct tape.

Welding mask

Cash

Bait

Time machine so you can escape into the distant past when this is all over.

•STEP TWO•
PLACE THE CAT INTO THE CARRIER

This is the tricky part.

Place both hands firmly on either side of your cat just below her shoulders. Hook your thumbs under her front legs and gently lead her into the carrier where . . .

If you have not lost too much blood, you may try talking to your cat with a soft, gentle, supportive tone of voice.

"Hi, Kitty. Aren't you a pretty, little kitty? Yes, you are! Yes, you are! Won't you be a good little, pretty kitty and go into the carrier? You are not well, my precious little jewel, and we need to take you to the nice doctor so you can feel better. Let me lead you into the carrier, my sweet, little, precious, little, pretty kitty cat so we can . . .

If the subtle method should fail (and it will), try using a strong, harsh tone of voice to let your cat know that YOU are the one in charge and that YOU should be taken seriously.

HEY, YOU!! YEAH, YOU!!!

DO YOU KNOW WHO I AM? I'M THE BOSS
AROUND HERE! THAT'S WHO! AND THAT MEANS
I'M IN CHARGE! I MAKE THE RULES!

SO IF I SAY "JUMP," YOU ASK ME "HOW HIGH?" AND IF I SAY "CRAWL ON YOUR BELLY," YOU ASK ME "FOR HOW LONG?" AND IF I SAY "GET IN THAT CARRIER," YOU . . .

If it appears that communication has completely broken down, you may want to try a different approach.

Try bribery.
LOOK, KITTY! I have a whole bag of delicious "dried octopus snacks" for you. It's yours if you'll just go into the carrier.

Mmmm! Do you smell that? Fresh catnip! You can have all you want if you'll just get into that carrier.
OH, COME ON! Pleeeeeeease!

I'll give you twenty dollars! Make it a hundred! Two hundred. Okay, FIVE HUNDRED DOLLARS, but that's my final offer!

*Sung to the tune of "Jingle Bells."

If all else fails. You can always use THE BAIT.

Hi, Puppy.

Puppy, would you mind stepping into that carrier over there? Thank you.

That was easy.

Hi, Kitty. Did I tell you that I happened to see Puppy eating all of your toys this morning? It's true. I watched him do it. He put all of your toys, one by one, into his mouth. And then he ate them. All of them. He especially ate all of your favorite toys.

He says they were delicious.

So, in conclusion, Kitty, all of your toys are now inside of Puppy. And Puppy? He is inside of this carrier.

IT WORKED!

PUPPY! GET OUT OF THERE! FAST!

I'm sorry, Puppy. I owe you.

QUICK!
SHUT THE DOOR!

Whew!

•STEP THREE•
TRANSPORTATION

Use fireplace tongs, a hockey stick, a crowbar, or any kind of long, sturdy pole to transport carrier with cat inside to vet. A police escort is optional, but highly recommended.

•STEP FOUR•
LOGIC

Ask yourself why you own a cat in the first place.

The following is a list of animals that will not try to murder you when you bring them to the vet.

Dog

Buffalo

Goldfish

Hamster

Tarantula

Komodo Dragon

Giant Squid

Guinea Pig

Vampire Bat

Pretty much every other animal in the world other than cats.

•STEP FIVE•
REPEAT

Repeat Step Four as often as necessary until you come to your senses and buy a gerbil.

UNCLE MURRAY'S FUN FACTS

WHAT IS A VETERINARIAN?

Someone who doesn't eat meat?

Essentially, a veterinarian—or "vet," for short—is a doctor for animals. But just as there are lots of different kinds of animals, there are different kinds of vets. Here are some of them.

• **Small Animal Vets**—These are the most common types of vets. They see cats and dogs and sometimes rabbits, guinea pigs, and even hamsters. These vets see common pets.

• **Exotic Animal Vets**—Some pets are not so common. Some people own hedgehogs or ferrets or snakes or parrots. These animals need a vet, too. And the exotic animal vets are there for them.

• What about farm animals? These animals are seen by the **Large Animal Vets**. These are the vets who do the most house calls because you can't bring a herd of cows or horses into a doctor's office. You could try. But it wouldn't be a good idea.

• Zoo animals? They're seen by **Wild Animal Vets**, of course. These vets have to be knowledgeable of a whole wide variety of unusual animals, from apes and bats to yaks and zebras.

• And lastly, there are the **Specialists**, vets who specialize their study and care in a single species of animal, like a cat, or even in a single body part, like a cat's heart. These doctors often do important research that helps all of the other vets take care of their patients.

Don't believe everything you read. Cats don't HAVE hearts!

The reason we're here, Doc, is because Kitty stopped eating all of a sudden and we just don't know why. We're all terribly worried.

LET'S MAKE KITTY SOUP!
DELICIOUS SOUP FOR
EATING! SOUP FOR OUR
HUNGRY BELLIES!

A FRESH, PLUMP KITTY IS JUST WHAT WE NEED FOR OUR SOUP! SOUP! SOUP FOR OUR SUPPER!

61

This is by far the most amazing thing I've ever seen.

67

UNCLE MURRAY'S FUN FACTS

WHAT DOES A VET DO?

A vet frets over pet threats!

A vet's job is very serious.

Sorry, again.

A vet's job is to keep your pet healthy. To do this, it's important that you do your part, too. Don't just bring your cat in to see the vet when she's sick. Just as you see your own doctor at least once a year for a checkup, your cat should go in just as often. And a vet will do everything your own doctor will do to make sure everything is normal.

The vet will use a scale to weigh your cat.

The vet will use a thermometer to check your cat's temperature.

The vet will use an otoscope to check inside your cat's ears and eyes.

The vet will use a stethoscope to listen to your cat's heart and lungs.

The vet will look inside your cat's mouth to see her teeth and peer down her throat. (Only your cat probably won't say "Ahhh!")

The vet will gently press down on and feel the area around your cat's belly to check for anything unusual.

And, yes, a vet will give your cat shots just like your doctor gives to you. Cats need vaccinations to prevent them from contracting certain serious diseases.

Your cat may not like these visits to the vet, but they're important. Every visit to the vet ensures that your cat will live a longer and healthier life.

Do cats get a sticker or a toy at the end of their appointments? Once I got a yo-yo!

•CHAPTER FOUR•
PUSSYCAT PARADISE

COME ON, KITTY!

COME ON!

JOURNEY
THROUGH THE
CAT DOOR FROM
YOUR WORLD
INTO THE NEXT!

NOW, STAND YE ON LINE, KITTY, FOR TODAY IS YOUR DAY OF JUDGMENT! DO NOT DESPAIR, FOR THE LINE IS LONG, BUT IT IS QUICK! HELP YE TO A COMPLIMENTARY FISH TREAT WHILE YE WAIT!

Let's see now . . . Thomas . . . Thomas . . . Ah, here you are! Hello, Thomas. So you ran into a wall while chasing a mouse. Too bad. Too bad, indeed. You'd be amazed by how often this happens. But I see that you have led an honorable life as a pussycat, so you may pass.

89

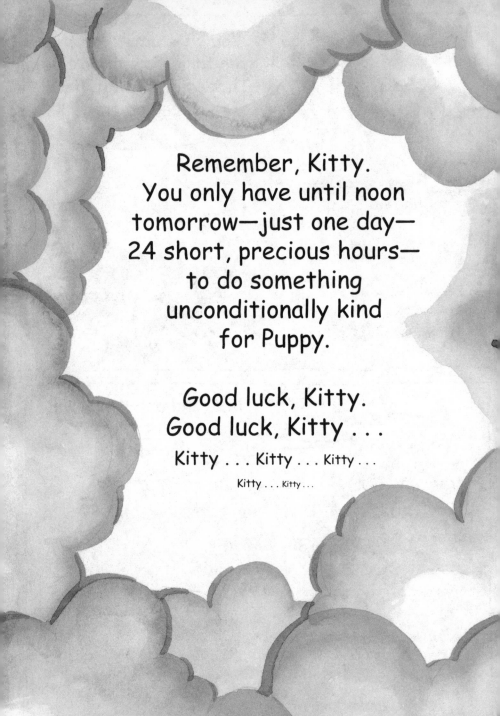

Remember, Kitty.
You only have until noon
tomorrow—just one day—
24 short, precious hours—
to do something
unconditionally kind
for Puppy.

Good luck, Kitty.
Good luck, Kitty . . .
Kitty . . . Kitty . . . Kitty . . .
Kitty . . . Kitty . . .

•CHAPTER FIVE•
HOME AGAIN

Kitty . . . Kitty . . . Wake up, Kitty. It's all over. You're home now and back from the vet.

All you had was a rotten tooth. The vet gave you a sedative and then yanked that tooth right out. That's a relief.

I'll bet you're pretty hungry now, Kitty. After all you've been asleep for almost an **ENTIRE DAY**.

That's right, Kitty. That sedative really knocked you out. To be honest, we were pretty worried that you might not . . . you know . . . that you might not wake up at all.

But I'm glad that you finally did wake up, Kitty. It's actually quite a relief. I know you like to sleep a lot, Kitty, but this time you've been asleep for almost **24 HOURS**.

I'll just go get you something to eat, Kitty. I'll be right back in a . . .

What is it, Kitty? What do you want?

101

Oh, PUPPY! You're looking for Puppy! Well, isn't that sweet. Puppy's been so worried about you ever since we brought you back from the vet.

Puppy's not here. We sent him over to Uncle Murray's house early this morning. We didn't want him to disturb you while you were sleeping.

THWAP!

But, don't worry, Kitty. Puppy should be home in a few hours. Gosh, it really is so nice that you actually seem to miss him. I never expected you to . . . HEY! Where are you going?

*Did you know that a cat can run as fast as 30 miles per hour, but only for a few seconds? That's just a bit faster than people and elephants, but not quite as fast as reindeer and giraffes.

107

Boy, do I know how you feel! Just last year I had a tooth yanked out because it had gone bad on me. See, I really like jelly beans, all kinds of jelly beans. I like the red ones, the blue ones, the yellow ones, the green ones, and even the black ones. Why, I bet if someone invented an eggplant jelly bean, I'd like it!

But my problem is that I don't brush my teeth like I should, and if you're going to eat jelly beans—any kind of candy, really—then you have to brush your teeth. I wonder if anyone's already invented an eggplant jelly bean. I should look into that. You know, if I ever form a band, I think I'll call it Eggplant Jelly Bean. That would be awesome! "WE ARE EGGPLANT JELLY BEAN, AND WE ARE HERE TO ROCK YOU!!"

Hey! Where'd you go?

109

113

WHINE?

117

119

GLOMP!

DOG TREATS

123

125

BONG

BONG

Sigh. That is truly disgusting. I feel like the floor of a movie theater. Maybe, Kitty, we haven't given you enough credit for your restraint.

133

COME ON, KITTY! COME ON!
It's time to wake up.
Wake up, you lazy old cat you.

Oh, good. You're awake. WHEW! We were starting to get worried. You've been asleep for about 24 hours now. That's a lot, even for you.

And I'll bet you're hungry NOW! It turns out that the only problem you had was a rotten tooth. The vet gave you a sedative and then yanked that bad tooth right out.

AND HERE COMES GOOD OL' PUPPY!

He's been so worried about you. He was howling and making a huge fuss because he thought you might never wake up again. Silly dog! He was making such a commotion that we had to send him over to Uncle Murray's house. He only just got back!

Anyway, you must be hungry, Kitty. So here's some lunch!

And as a special treat, we also made your favorite dessert: liver and kidney pie with an extra large helping of whipped cream on top.

BUT you have to share some of that pie with Puppy. Do you hear me, Kitty? You have to **SHARE!**

THE END